A Note to Parents and Caregivers:

With a focus on math, science, and social studies, *Read-it!* Readers support both the learning of content information and the extension of more complex reading skills. They encourage the development of problem-solving skills that help children expand their thinking.

 The PURPLE LEVEL presents basic topics and objects using high frequency words and simple language patterns.

 The RED LEVEL presents familiar topics using common words and repeating sentence patterns.

 The BLUE LEVEL presents new ideas using a larger vocabulary and varied sentence structure.

 The YELLOW LEVEL presents more challenging ideas, a broad vocabulary, and wide variety in sentence structure.

 The GREEN LEVEL presents more complex ideas, an extended vocabulary range, and expanded language structures.

 The ORANGE LEVEL presents a wide range of ideas and concepts using challenging vocabulary and complex language structures.

When sharing a content focused book with your child, read to find out facts and concepts, pausing often to restate and talk about the new information. The realistic story format provides an opportunity to talk about the language used, and to learn about reading to problem-solve for information. Encourage children to measure, make maps, and consider other situations that allow them to apply what they are learning.

There is no right or wrong way to share books with children. Find time to read and share new learning with your child, and pass on the legacy of literacy.

Adria F. Klein, Ph.D.
Professor Emeritus
California State University
San Bernardino, California

Editor: Julie Gassman
Designer: Hilary Wacholz
Art Director: Heather Kindseth
Managing Editor: Christianne Jones
The illustrations in this book were created with gouache, colored pencil,
and cold press paper.

Picture Window Books
151 Good Counsel Drive
P.O. Box 669
Mankato, MN 56002-0669
877-845-8392
www.picturewindowbooks.com

Printed in the United States of America.

Library of Congress Cataloging-in-Publication Data
Blackaby, Susan.
Water wise/ by Susan Blackaby; illustrated by Susan DeSantis.
p. cm. — (Read-it! readers. Science)
Includes bibliographical references.
ISBN 978-1-4048-5260-0
[1. Water conservation—Fiction.] I. DeSantis, Susan, 1964- ill. II. Title.
PZ7.B5318Wat 2009
[E]—dc22
                                     2008032415

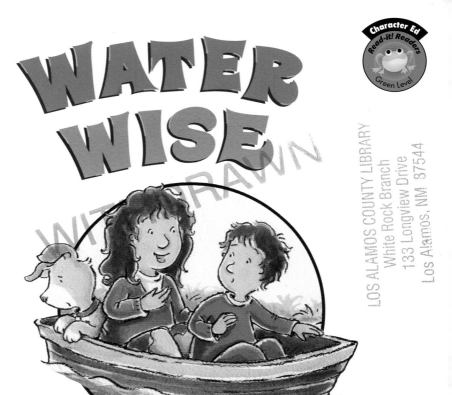

WATER WISE

by Susan Blackaby
illustrated by Susan DeSantis

Special thanks to our advisers for their expertise:

Wei Lin, Ph.D.
Director, Environmental and Conservation Sciences Graduate Program
North Dakota State University

Adria F. Klein, Ph.D.
Professor Emeritus, California State University
San Bernardino, California

PICTURE WINDOW BOOKS
Minneapolis, Minnesota

Kelly could not get a wink of sleep. A soft noise was keeping her awake.

Drip. Drip. Drip.

She went down the hall to the bathroom. The faucet was dripping. Kelly turned the faucet tight.

The dripping stopped. Kelly went back to bed.

The next day, Kelly heard the soft drips again. "Why is the faucet dripping again?" Kelly wondered.

She turned the faucet tight.
The dripping stopped.

When Kelly came upstairs later, she heard water gushing.

"Now what?" Kelly wondered.

In the bathroom she found her brother, Jack, at the sink.

Kelly turned off the water.

"Hey, I was brushing my teeth," said Jack.

"No you weren't," said Kelly. "You were wasting water. Get your brush wet. Then turn the water off until you need to rinse."

Jack finished brushing his teeth. He rinsed his toothbrush. Then he turned off the water.

"Jack, you have to make sure the water is all the way off," said Kelly. "Otherwise the faucet drips."

"So what?" said Jack.

"It wastes water," said Kelly.

"It is just one little drop," said Jack.

"Little drops add up," said Kelly. "I'll show you."

Kelly plugged up the sink. Pretty soon the drops made a little puddle.

"See that?" Kelly said. "If we let this keep dripping, soon the sink would overflow. The bathroom could flood. Water could gush out the door and into the hall."

Jack looked surprised. "That's a lot of water," he said.

"That's right," said Kelly. "In a week, one leaky faucet can waste 50 gallons of water. That is enough to fill up a bathtub."

Kelly turned off the faucet to stop the drip. Jack flicked the water with his finger.

"Dinosaurs once swam in that water," said Kelly.

Jack thought Kelly must be teasing,
but he was not sure.

"They did?" he asked.

"Yes, they did," said Kelly.

"This water flowed down the Nile River when the pyramids were being built," she added.

"Christopher Columbus sailed to the Americas in it," she said.

"What do you mean?" said Jack.

"That water has been flowing around the Earth for millions of years," said Kelly. "Every drop of water on Earth is part of the water cycle."

"Water goes from the ocean to the air to the land. Then it starts all over again," she added.

"So the water cycle keeps going and going?" asked Jack.

"It never stops," said Kelly.

Jack reached for the faucet and turned on the water.

"Now what are you doing?" said Kelly.

"I'm getting a drink," said Jack. "All this water talk is making me thirsty!"

Jack filled up his water bottle. Then he turned off the faucet. He made sure it was good and tight.

"Lucky for me there is a whole ocean of water, in case I need more," said Jack.

"If you need to drink the ocean, you are out of luck," said Kelly. "There is a lot of water on Earth, but most of it is either frozen or salty. Just a little bit can be used for drinking. That is why it is important to keep it clean and not waste it."

Kelly and Jack went downstairs.
Jack filled their dog Freddie's water dish.

"Here, Freddie," said Jack. "Have some Dinosaur Juice. Try not to splash with that big tongue of yours. You shouldn't waste a drop."

"You got that right," said Kelly. "If everyone in the United States used just a little bit less water, we would save gallons and gallons and gallons. That includes you, too, Freddie."

That night, Kelly hopped into bed. She heard a soft, steady noise.

Drip. Drip. Drip.

Raindrops were hitting the roof. They dripped onto the ground. Kelly closed her eyes. She smiled. Then she fell asleep.

Poster Activity

A poster is a great way to share information with other people. Make a poster about saving water.

What you need:
- A piece of poster board
- Markers, stickers and other items

What to do:
1. Find out how much water people use every day.
2. Use this information to suggest ways people can cut their water use. How much water can a family save in a week?
3. Include what you've learned on your poster. Make up a slogan, illustrate your ideas, and decorate your poster.

Glossary

gallon—U.S. unit of measurement for volume equal to 3.79 liters

water cycle—the constant movement of the Earth's water; water from rivers and oceans rises into the air as a gas, forms clouds, then falls as rain or snow to fill the rivers and oceans again

To Learn More

More Books to Read

Sam Godwin. *The Drop Goes Plop.* Minneapolis, Minn.: Picture Window Books, 2005.

Sara E. Nelson. *Let's Save Water.* Mankato, Minn.: Capstone Press, 2007.

Guillain, Charlotte. *Saving Water.* Chicago, Ill.: Heinemann Library, 2008.

On the Web

FactHound offers a safe, fun way to find Web sites related to topics in this book. All of the sites on FactHound have been researched by our staff.

1. Visit *www.facthound.com*
2. Type in this special code: 1404852603
3. Click on the FETCH IT button.

Your trusty FactHound will fetch the best sites for you!

Look for more books in the *Read-it!* Readers: Science series:

The Autumn Leaf (Earth science: seasons)
The Busy Spring (Earth science: seasons)
The Cold Winter Day (Earth science: seasons)
Friends and Flowers (life science: bulbs)
The Grass Patch Project (life science: grass)
Jenna and the Three R's (Earth science: recycling)
The Moving Carnival (physical science: motion)
A Secret Matter (physical science: matter)
A Stormy Surprise (physical science: electricity)
The Summer Playground (Earth science: seasons)
The Sunflower Farmer (life science: sunflowers)
Surprising Beans (life science: beans)
Up, Up in the Air (physical science: air)

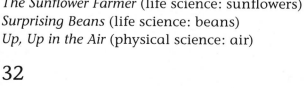